292 OSB	Osborne, Mary Pope. Favorite Greek myths.	10381

$13.56

DATE DUE	BORROWER'S NAME	ROOM NO.

10381

292
OSB

Osborne, Mary Pope.

Favorite Greek
myths.

**GEORGETOWN ELEM SCHOOL LMC
DISTRICT 204**

873581 01356   05610C   02

FAVORITE GREEK MYTHS

FAVORITE GREEK MYTHS

RETOLD BY
MARY POPE OSBORNE

ILLUSTRATED BY
TROY HOWELL

SCHOLASTIC INC.

NEW YORK

Grateful acknowledgment is made to Indiana University Press
for permission to quote from *Metamorphoses* by Ovid,
translated by Rolfe Humphries, 1955.

Library of Congress Cataloging-in-Publication Data

Osborne, Mary Pope.
Favorite Greek Myths.

Summary: Retells twelve tales from Greek
mythology, including the stories of King Midas,
Echo and Narcissus, the Golden Apples, and Cupid
and Psyche.
1. Mythology, Greek—Juvenile literature.
[1. Mythology, Greek]   I. Howell, Troy, ill.
II. Title.
BL782.O86   1989   292'.13   87-32332
ISBN 0-590-41338-4

12 11 10 9 8 7 6 5 4   0 1 2 3 4/9

Printed in the U.S.A.   36

First Scholastic printing, May 1989
Designed by Claire Counihan

For MICHAEL, BECCA, and
NATHANIEL
M.P.O.

To DAVID GRAHAM:
He that has light within his own cleer brest
May sit i'th center and enjoy bright day

(from *Comus* by John Milton)
T.H.

CONTENTS

CONTENTS

INTRODUCTION

WELCOME to a strange and beautiful world where human forms turn into seagulls, lions, bears, and stars. Welcome to a world where the impossible seems common; where the moon, the sun, and the wind are all gods. Welcome to the world of Greek mythology.

Imagine yourself living on an ancient Greek island, before the days of airplanes, cars, and television — when civilization was very young, and people lived very close to nature. How would you have explained such mysteries of the earth as weather changes, or where rainbows come from, or why spiders spin webs?

The ancient Greeks invented stories to help explain nature and to free them from their fears of the unknown. When the sun rose in the sky, it meant the sun god was driving his golden chariot through the heavens. When winter turned to spring, it meant a young goddess had just returned to earth to live with her mother. When lightning flashed, it meant the god of the skies was hurling his thunderbolts in anger.

The stories the ancient Greeks created about their gods and goddesses are called myths. Not only did the myths help explain the mysteries of nature, but they also provided wonderful entertainment on cold winter nights. As the myths were passed from generation to generation, different Greek and Roman poets retold them.

Nearly all of the myths in this collection are derived from the work of the Roman poet Ovid, who lived 2,000 years ago. Ovid's book, *Metamorphoses*, tells about the mortals of earth and the gods and goddesses who lived on Mount Olympus, a mysterious mountaintop above Greece. In nearly all of Ovid's stories, the gods or mortals change into different shapes and forms.

Though today we may have more modern ideas about life than the ancient Greeks or Romans did, our feelings are still much the same as theirs. As we read about their gods, goddesses, and mortals romping through woods and over mountains and seas, we understand their sorrows, joys, and angers. Welcome to their world — one that is as lively and passionate today as it was long ago.

"My intention is to tell
of bodies changed to different forms;
the gods, who made the changes will help me,
or so I hope,
with a poem that runs from the world's beginnings
to our own days."

—Ovid's *Metamorphoses*

FAVORITE
GREEK
MYTHS

CHARIOT
OF THE SUN GOD

The Story of Phaeton and Helios

HAETON entered the gleaming palace of the sun god and walked to the throne room. He stopped in the doorway, blinded by the radiance of Helios, the sun god, who wore a purple robe and sat high on a throne of emeralds. Around Helios stood his attendants, whose names were Day, Month, Year, Century, Hours, Spring, Summer, Autumn, and Winter.

"Come to me, my boy," said Helios, the sun god.

Phaeton stepped forward and bowed his head to shield his eyes from the sun's awesome brightness. Then he kneeled before the throne.

"What brings you to seek your father?" Helios asked gently.

"I came to get your promise that I am really your son," Phaeton answered. "The boys at school laugh at me and say I'm not, but my mother has always said my father is the sun."

"Clymene is right," said Helios. "The nymph Clymene had a child by me, and it was you. To prove I'm your father, I'll give you anything you ask. I swear it by Styx, the river of oaths."

"Father, I've only one wish. I want to do what you do early

each morning. I want to drive your fiery chariot alone across the sky and turn night into day."

"Oh, no! I cannot allow you to do that!" cried Helios.

"But you promised — "

"I spoke too rashly! Please, may the gods allow me to take back my promise!"

"It's too late, Father!" said Phaeton.

"But this is the one wish I cannot grant, my son! The trip is too dangerous. Even Jupiter — greatest of all the gods — cannot drive my winged horses! They're hot with fire!"

"I can drive them, Father. If I'm really your son."

"No! You can't! How can you fight the spin of the world? How can you fight the wild beasts and the terrible monsters?"

But Phaeton only smiled at Helios. "I know I can do what you do, Father," he said.

The sun god tried to stall for time, but the goddess Dawn was coming quickly upon the palace, getting ready to throw open her crimson doors and to shine forth. The moon's thin crescent had vanished from sight; the stars had taken flight. It was time for Helios's fiery chariot to begin its daily course across the sky.

Helios and Phaeton stepped out into the cool air where the chariot waited. The gleaming cart had tires of gold and spokes of silver, and every jewel imaginable sparkled in the rosy light of the early morning.

As Phaeton walked around the golden chariot, marveling at its beauty, his father tried to think of ways to stop him from taking the terrible journey across the sky.

But when birds began singing, Phaeton cried, "I must leave now, Father!" And he jumped into the shining chariot.

The four winged horses stamped their hooves and breathed fire from their nostrils as two goddesses, both named Hours, fastened their jingling harnesses.

The sun god rubbed a magic salve on Phaeton's face to shield him from the heat. He set his crown of flashing sunbeams on the boy's head. Then he looked at his son and sighed. "At least listen to my advice," he said. "Keep to the middle path. Do not veer off to the side! Neither get too high nor too low, for the sky and earth need equal heat. If you're too high, you'll burn the sky, and if you're too low, you'll burn the earth —"

"All right, Father!" cried Phaeton as he held the reins proudly, and the horses neighed and pawed the ground.

"Follow the wheel tracks of my daily path!" cried Helios. "Spare the whip and hold the reins tightly!"

"I will, Father! I will!"

"And beware of the northern bear and the twisting snake in the sky —"

Before the sun god could say more, Phaeton snapped the reins. "It's time, Father!" he said. "Day's calling! Night is gone!"

Suddenly the four horses leapt forward into the boundless sky.

"Don't go, my son!" shouted Helios. "Let *me* give the world light today!"

But Phaeton couldn't hear his father. The swift hooves of his horses ripped open the clouds. Then the winged steeds soared higher and higher into the sky.

The chariot was so light, it tossed back and forth like a ship on stormy waves. The horses grew frightened and galloped faster — until they were more swift than the East Wind. Phaeton pulled hard on the reins, but he couldn't slow his horses down. He looked around wildly, but he couldn't see the wheel tracks — the horses had left their worn path!

As he wheeled off course, Phaeton's sunbeams warmed the constellations: The Snake stirred from its icy numbness. The Great Bear woke in a rage and began lumbering about the heavens.

Phaeton looked below, and when he realized how far away the earth was he became sick with fright. He called in panic for his father's help. He yelled for his horses to stop, but the horses galloped out of control. They swept past more savage beasts in the sky — past the giant scorpion that sweated black venom as its curved stinger reached out toward the fiery chariot.

Phaeton dropped the reins, and the horses bounded into regions they'd never traveled before. They crashed into stars. All of heaven cried out in terror as the fiery chariot careened off course. The moon, the skies, and the earth all caught fire. Flames spread across mountaintops and burned the snow, spilling black smoke into the clouds. Even Mount Olympus, home of the gods, was besieged with fire.

Then Phaeton saw the earth set aflame. Everything glowed white-hot: the deserts, woodland pools, and springs. Everyone on earth was trying to escape the great fire. The gods of the underworld and even the sea nymphs in their deep ocean caves felt the searing heat.

Mother Earth shielded her hot forehead and shuddered in agony. Burdened with flame, she cried out to Jupiter, the greatest of the gods: "Hurl your lightning bolts now and end this fiery death caused by Phaeton!" Then she could speak no longer, for the smoke and flames were choking her.

Jupiter, hypnotized by the sight of flames licking the world, roused himself when he saw Mother Earth dying. He rolled his thunder, then lifted a giant bolt of lightning behind his head and flung it through the sky. The bolt struck the sun chariot, breaking its wheel and spokes — and fire extinguished fire, flame put out flame, and the mad horses leapt free of their harnesses as Phaeton fell from the sky.

Phaeton's hair was on fire as he fell. Leaving behind a trail of sparks, he looked like a falling star. Far from home, half a world away from his mother, he fell into a river.

The river god held Phaeton's poor, smoldering body and bathed his burning face. Then the water nymphs buried Phaeton; and on his tomb, they wrote:

"Here lies Phaeton who tried to be the sun.
Greatly he failed, but greatly he dared."

For a whole day the sun god mourned his son. He refused to drive his chariot — and the men and women on earth had to burn fires to gain light and warmth.

When Jupiter went to see the sun god, he found him sitting on his emerald throne with his head bowed, not moving as he sat in mourning. Jupiter bid Helios to look up and answer to him for not driving his golden chariot.

But Helios cursed the god of the skies for throwing his thunderbolt and killing Phaeton.

"I had no choice!" said mighty Jupiter. "The boy's ambition nearly ended the world. Mother Earth was burning and dying. But now she is too cold, Helios. She needs your heat, or she will die from freezing."

The sun god bowed his head further.

"Rise, Helios!" roared Jupiter. "Stop blaming me for your son's death! You have work to do! The world is waiting for you!"

The sun god heaved a great sigh, then slowly rose from his throne. Trembling with sorrow, he strode out of his palace.

The four winged horses who had leapt free from Phaeton were

snuffling in the cool early air, stamping their hooves as Dawn opened her crimson doors.

The sun god stepped into the gleaming golden chariot. He put on his crown of flashing sunbeams — the same crown Phaeton had worn. Then the two goddesses of Hours yoked the four winged horses with jingling harnesses. And as the weeping sun god grabbed the reins tightly and snapped them, they bolted into the boundless, blue, sunlit sky.

THE GOLDEN TOUCH
The Story of Bacchus
and King Midas

BACCHUS, the merry god of the vine, raised his goblet. "To you, King Midas," he said, "and because you have been so hospitable to me — ask for anything you wish, and I will grant it to you."

"What an idea!" said Midas. "Anything I wish?"

"Indeed, anything," said Bacchus.

"Anything?"

"Yes! Yes!"

"Ah, well," said the king, chuckling. "Of course, there's only one thing: I wish that everything I touch would turn to gold!" Midas looked sideways at Bacchus, for he couldn't believe such a gift could really be his.

"My friend, you already have all the gold you could possibly want," said Bacchus, looking disappointed.

"Oh, no! I don't!" said Midas. "One never has enough gold!"

"Well, if that's what you wish for, I suppose I will have to grant it," said Bacchus.

Bacchus soon took his leave. As Midas waved good-bye to him, his hand brushed an oak twig hanging from a tree — and the twig turned to gold!

The king screamed with joy, then shouted after Bacchus, "My wish has come true! Thank you! Thank you!"

The god turned and waved, then disappeared down the road.

Midas looked around excitedly. He leaned over and picked a stone up from the ground — and the stone turned into a golden nugget! He kicked the sand — and the sand turned to golden grains!

King Midas threw back his head and shouted, "I'm the richest man in the world!" Then he rushed about his grounds, touching everything. And everything, *everything* turned to gold: ears of corn in his fields! Apples plucked from trees! The pillars of his mansion!

When the king's servants heard him shouting, they rushed to see what was happening. They found their king dancing wildly on his lawn, turning the grass to glittering blades of gold. Everyone laughed and clapped as Midas washed his hands in his fountain and turned the water to a gleaming spray!

Finally, exhausted but overjoyed, King Midas called for his dinner. His servants placed a huge banquet meal before him on his lawn. "Oh, I'm so hungry!" he said as he speared a piece of meat and brought it to his mouth.

But suddenly King Midas realized his wish may not have been as wonderful as he thought — for the moment he bit down on the meat, it, too, turned to gold.

Midas laughed uneasily, then reached for a piece of bread. But as soon as his hands touched the bread, it also became a hard, golden nugget! Weak with dread, Midas reached for his goblet of water. But alas! His lips touched only hard, cold metal. The water had also turned to gold.

Covering his head and moaning, King Midas realized his great wish was going to kill him. He would starve to death or die of thirst!

"Bacchus!" he cried, throwing his hands toward heaven. "I've been a greedy fool! Take away your gift! Free me from my golden touch! Help me, Bacchus!"

The sobbing king fell off his chair to his knees. He beat his fists against the ground, turning even the little anthills to gold. His servants grieved for him, but none dared go near him, for they feared he might accidently turn them to gold, too!

As everyone wailed with sorrow, Bacchus suddenly appeared on the palace lawn. The merry god stood before the sobbing king for a moment, then said, "Rise, Midas."

Stumbling to his feet, King Midas begged Bacchus to forgive him and to take away the curse of the golden touch.

"You were greedy and foolish, my friend," said Bacchus. "But I will forgive you. Now go and wash yourself in the Pactolus River that runs by Sardis, and you'll be cleansed of this desire to have more gold than anyone else!"

King Midas did as Bacchus said. He washed in the Pactolus, leaving behind streams of gold in the river's sands. Then he returned home and happily ate his dinner.

LOST AT SEA

The Story of Ceyx
and Alcyone

KING Ceyx, son of the morning star, walked along the shore with his wife, Alcyone, daughter of the king of the winds.

"I must leave in a few days on a long sea voyage and travel to the Oracle of Delphi," King Ceyx told his wife. "But I promise I will be gone for no more than two months."

Alcyone turned pale. She knew the rough winds in the open seas were very dangerous. "My father, Aeolus, rules the winds — I know what force he can unleash in a bad storm. I beg you, if you love me, don't go!"

King Ceyx assured Alcyone of his love for her and promised to return soon, but she would not be consoled. A few days later, when he stood in the stern of his ship and waved good-bye, she flung herself down on the sands and wept bitterly. Then she dragged herself home and began her long wait for her husband's return.

One night, as King Ceyx's ship sailed upon the open sea, the waves began rising. "Pull in your oars! Lower the sails!" the captain shouted.

But the men could not hear him, for the winds had begun to howl, and thunder rumbled in the sky. Ocean spray leapt for the stars, as lightning lit the night. Then the sea turned yellow, and the heavens poured water in great torrents, as waves crashed in on the king's ship.

Ceyx's last thoughts were of Alcyone. He cried to the gods, "Wash my body to my wife over the sea!" And he called her name again and again, until a great arc of water took him down to the dark depths of the ocean. And then there was no more lightning and no more starlight; everything was pitch-black.

The morning star did not shine the next day, but hid behind the clouds, grieving for his drowned son.

Alcyone was counting the days until Ceyx returned. She wove a beautiful robe for him and a dress for herself to wear when he came home. Every day she burned incense and prayed to Juno, the goddess who protects married women, asking her to bring her husband home safely.

Hearing Alcyone's prayers, Juno felt pity. Finally she summoned her messenger, Iris, the rainbow goddess. She instructed Iris to travel to the god Sleep and ask Sleep to send Alcyone a dream, telling her that her husband had drowned at sea.

Iris took off at once, trailing her thousand colors across the sky, until she touched down upon the twilight lands of the Cimmerian country. There the god Sleep lived in the hollow of a mountain. When Iris arrived at Sleep's cave, she heard no birds singing or dogs barking or geese cackling. Only the river, Lethe, whispered sleepily in the twilight as Iris stepped past poppy beds and entered Sleep's cave.

The rainbow goddess pushed aside the empty dreams in her way, then came upon Sleep, snoring in a great ebony bed. Iris awakened the slumbering god and bid him send a dream to Alcyone. After Sleep agreed, Iris soared back to Mount Olympus, trailing her rainbow colors across the sky.

Sleep roused Morpheus, one of his thousand sons, the one who could best imitate humans. He instructed Morpheus to fly to Alcyone. Then the god returned to his bed, letting his drowsy head sink down again into the land of dreams.

On silent wings, Morpheus took off through the twilight. When he finally came to the home of Alcyone, he assumed the face and body of King Ceyx. He slipped into Alcyone's chamber and stood before her bed.

Ceyx's ghostly beard dripped with sea water, and tears ran down his face as he bent over his sleeping wife and whispered, "Oh, my love, do you see me? Have I changed in death? Cherish no hope for my return. My ship went down in a storm far out at sea, and I died, calling your name. Arise now and weep for me."

In her sleep, Alcyone wept and tried to take her husband into her arms, but it was no use. She clutched the air and cried out for him, until her own voice woke her. Alcyone realized she'd been dreaming, but fearing her dream might have been the truth, she wept until dawn.

When light crept into her bedroom chamber, Alcyone rose and slipped down to the shore, to the place where she had last seen Ceyx, standing in the stern of his boat, waving to her.

As she stared at the sea, Alcyone spotted something floating on the water. She stepped closer and saw a man's body on top of the waves. "Oh, poor sailor," she said, "and poor wife, if you're married."

When the waves washed the body closer to shore, Alcyone saw it was her husband. She cried out, "Oh, my love! Why have you come back to me this way?"

Then she rushed into the sea. And though the waves broke against her, she did not go under. Instead, she began beating the water with giant wings. Then, crying out like a bird, she rose into the air and flew over the sea to Ceyx's lifeless body. When she touched her husband's cold lips with her beak, he also became a bird, and the two of them were together again.

Since that time, every year, for seven days before the winter solstice, the waves are quiet, and the water is perfectly calm. These days are called *halcyon days*, for during them, the king of the winds keeps the wind at home — because his daughter, Alcyone, is brooding on her nest upon the sea.

THE WEAVING CONTEST

The Story of Arachne and Minerva

ARACHNE, a proud peasant girl, was a wonderful spinner and weaver of wool. The water nymphs journeyed from their rivers and the wood nymphs from their forests just to watch Arachne steep her wool in crimson dyes, then take the long threads in her skillful fingers and weave exquisite tapestries.

"Ah! Minerva must have given you your gift!" declared a wood nymph one day. Minerva was the goddess of weaving and handicrafts.

Arachne threw back her head. "Ha! Minerva has taught me nothing! I've taught myself everything I know!" And with that, she decided to challenge Minerva to a contest. "Let's see which of us should be called 'goddess of the loom'!" she said.

The nymphs covered their mouths, frightened to hear such scorn heaped upon a powerful goddess of Mount Olympus.

Their fears were justified — for Minerva herself was furious when word got back to her about Arachne's conceit. The goddess immediately donned the disguise of an old woman with gray hair and hobbled with a cane to Arachne's cottage.

When Arachne opened her door, Minerva shook her gnarled

finger. "If I were you," said the old woman, "I would not compare myself so favorably to the great goddess Minerva. I would feel humble toward her and ask her to pardon my prideful arrogance."

"You silly fool!" said Arachne. "What do you mean by coming to my door and telling me what to do? If that goddess is half so great as the world thinks, let her come here and show me!"

"She is here!" boomed a powerful voice, and before Arachne's eyes, the old woman instantly changed into the goddess Minerva.

Arachne's face flushed with shame. Nevertheless she remained defiant and plunged headlong toward her doom. "Hello, Minerva," she said. "Do you dare to finally weave against me?"

Minerva only glared at the girl, as the nymphs, peeking from behind the trees, cringed to watch such insolence.

"Come in if you like," Arachne said, stepping back from her doorway and bidding the goddess to enter.

Without speaking, Minerva went into the cottage. Servants quickly dashed about, setting up two looms. Then Arachne and Minerva tucked up their long dresses and set to work. Their busy fingers flew back and forth as they each wove rainbows of colors: dark purples, pinks, golds, and crimsons.

Minerva wove a tapestry showing the twelve greatest gods and goddesses of Mount Olympus. But Arachne wove a tapestry showing not only the gods and goddesses, but their adventures also. Then she bordered her magnificent work with flowers and ivy.

The river nymphs and wood nymphs stared in awe at Arachne's tapestry. Her work was clearly better than Minerva's. Even the goddess Envy who haughtily inspected it, said, "There is no flaw."

When she heard Envy's words, Minerva lost her temper. The goddess tore Arachne's tapestry and hit her mercilessly — until disgraced and humiliated, Arachne crawled away and tried to hang herself.

At last, moved to a little pity, Minerva, said, "You may live, Arachne, but you will hang forever — and do your weaving in the air!"

Then the vengeful goddess sprinkled Arachne with hellbane; and the girl's hair fell off, and her nose and ears fell off. Her head shrank to a tiny size until she was mostly a giant belly. But her fingers could still weave; and within minutes, Arachne, the first spider on earth, wove the first magnificent web.

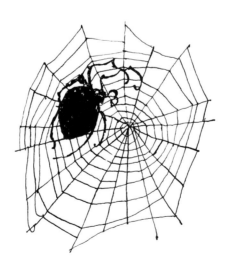

APOLLO'S TREE

The Story of Daphne
and Apollo

NE day when Apollo, the god of light and truth, was a young man, he came upon Cupid, the god of love, playing with one of his bows. "What are you doing with my bow?" Apollo asked angrily. "Don't try to steal my glory, Cupid! I've slain a great serpent with that weapon. Play with your own little bow and arrows!"

"Your arrows may slay serpents, Apollo," said the god of love, "but *my* arrows can do worse harm! Even you can be wounded by them!"

With that ominous threat, Cupid flew into the sky and landed on top of a high mountain. Then he pulled two arrows from his quiver: One had a blunt tip filled with lead. Whomever was hit by this arrow would run from anyone professing love. The second arrow was sharp and made of gold. Whomever was hit with this arrow would instantly fall in love.

Cupid aimed his first arrow at Daphne, a beautiful nymph hunting deep in the woods. Daphne was a follower of Diana, Apollo's twin sister and the goddess of wild things. Like Diana, Daphne loved her freedom, as she roamed the woods and fields with her hair in wild disarray and her limbs bare to the sun and rain.

Cupid pulled the bowstring back and shot the blunt-tipped arrow at Daphne. When the arrow flew through the air, it became invisible. And when it pierced Daphne's heart, she felt a sharp pain, but knew not why.

Holding her hands over her wound, Daphne rushed to her father, the river god. "Father!" she shouted. "You must make me a promise!"

"What is it?" called the god who stood in the river, surrounded by water nymphs.

"Promise I will never have to get married!" Daphne cried.

The river god, confused by his daughter's frantic request, called back, "But I wish to have grandchildren!"

"No, Father! No! I *never* want to get married! Please, let me always be as free as Diana!"

"But I want you to marry!" cried the god.

"No!" screamed Daphne. And she beat the water with her fists, then rocked back and forth and sobbed.

"All right!" shouted the river god. "Do not grieve so, Daphne! I promise I'll never make you marry!"

"And promise you'll help me escape my suitors!" cried the huntress.

"I promise, I will!" called the river god.

After Daphne secured this promise from her father, Cupid aimed his second arrow — the sharp, gold-tipped one — at Apollo, who was wandering in the woods. Just as the young god came upon Daphne, Cupid pulled back the tight string of his bow and shot the golden arrow into Apollo's heart.

The god instantly fell in love with Daphne. Even though the huntress's hair was wild and she wore only rough animal skins,

Apollo thought she was the most beautiful woman he'd ever seen.

"Hello!" he cried. But Daphne gave him a startled look, then bolted into the woods like a deer.

Apollo ran after her, shouting, "Stay! Stay!" But Daphne fled as fast as the wind.

"Don't run, please!" cried Apollo. "You flee like a dove flees an eagle. But I'm not your enemy! Don't run from me!"

Daphne continued to run.

"Stop!" Apollo cried.

Daphne did not slow down.

"Do you know who I am?" said the god. "I am not a farm boy or a shepherd. I am Lord of Delphi! Son of Jupiter! I've slain a great serpent with my arrow! But alas, I fear Cupid's weapons have wounded me worse!"

Daphne continued to run, her bare limbs lit by the sun and her soft hair wild in the wind.

Apollo grew tired of begging her to stop, so he began to pick up speed. On the wings of love, running more swiftly than he'd ever run before, the god of light and truth gave the girl no rest, until soon he was close upon her.

Her strength gone, Daphne could feel Apollo's breath on her hair. "Help me, Father!" she cried to the river god. "Help me!"

No sooner had she spoken these words, than her arms and legs grew heavy and turned to wood. Then her hair became leaves, and her feet became roots growing deep into the ground. She had become a laurel tree; and nothing was left of her, but her exquisite loveliness.

Apollo embraced the tree's branches as if they were Daphne's arms. He kissed her wooden flesh. Then he pressed his hands against the tree's trunk and wept.

"I feel your heart beating beneath this bark," Apollo said, tears running down his face. "Since you can't be my wife, you'll be my sacred tree. I'll use your wood for my harp and for my arrows. I'll weave your branches into a wreath for my head. Heroes and scholars will be crowned with your leaves. You'll always be young and green — my first love, Daphne."

THE FACE
IN THE POOL

The Story of Echo and Narcissus

WHEN Jupiter came to the mountains, the wood nymphs rushed to embrace the jovial god. They played with him in icy waterfalls and laughed with him in lush green glades.

Jupiter's wife, Juno, was very jealous, and often she searched the mountainside, trying to catch her husband with the nymphs. But whenever Juno came close to finding Jupiter, a charming nymph named Echo stepped across her path. Echo chatted with Juno in a lively fashion and did whatever she could to stall the goddess until Jupiter and the other nymphs had escaped.

Eventually Juno discovered that Echo had been tricking her, and she flew into a rage. "Your tongue has made a fool of me!" she shouted at Echo. "Henceforth, your voice will be more brief, my dear! You will always have the *last* word — but never the *first*!"

From that day on, poor Echo could only repeat the last words of what others said.

One day Echo spied a golden-haired youth hunting deer in the woods. The boy's name was Narcissus, and he was the most beautiful young man in the forest. All who looked upon Narcissus fell in love with him immediately. But he would have nothing to do with anyone, for he was very conceited.

When Echo first laid eyes on Narcissus, her heart burned like the flame of a torch. She secretly followed him through the woods, loving him more with each step. She got closer and closer until finally Narcissus heard the leaves rustling. He whirled around and cried out, "Who's here?"

From behind a tree, Echo repeated his last word, "Here!"

Narcissus looked about in wonder. "Who are you? Come to me!" he said.

"Come to me!" said Echo.

Narcissus searched the woods, but could not find the nymph. "Stop hiding! Let us meet!" he shouted.

"Let us meet!" Echo cried. Then she stepped from behind the tree and rushed to embrace Narcissus.

But the youth panicked when the nymph flung her arms around his neck. He pushed her away and shouted, "Leave me alone! I'd rather die than let you love me!"

"Love me!" was all poor Echo could say as she watched Narcissus run from her through the woods. "Love me! Love me! Love me!"

Humilated and filled with sorrow, Echo wandered the mountains until she found a lonely cave to live in.

Meanwhile Narcissus hunted in the woods, tending only to himself, until one day he discovered a hidden pool of water. The pool had a silvery-smooth surface. No shepherds ever disturbed its waters — no goats or cattle, no birds or fallen leaves. Only the sun danced upon the still pool.

Tired from hunting and eager to quench his thirst, Narcissus lay on his stomach and leaned over the water. But when he looked at the glassy surface, he saw someone staring back at him.

Narcissus was spellbound. Gazing up at him from the pool were eyes like twin stars, framed by hair as golden as Apollo's and cheeks as smooth as ivory. But when he leaned down and tried to kiss the perfect lips, he kissed only spring water. When he reached out and tried to embrace this vision of beauty, he found no one there.

"What love could be more cruel than this?" he cried. "When my lips kiss my beloved, they touch only water! When I reach for my beloved, I hold only water!"

Narcissus began to weep. When he wiped away his tears, the person in the water also wiped away tears. "Oh, no," sobbed Narcissus. "I see the truth now: It is *myself* I weep for! I yearn for my own reflection!"

As Narcissus cried harder, his tears broke the glassy surface of the pool and caused his reflection to disappear. "Come back! Where did you go?" the youth cried. "I love you so much! At least stay and let me look upon you!"

Day after day, Narcissus stared at the water, in love with his own reflection. He began to waste away from grief, until one sad morning, he felt himself dying. "Good-bye, my love!" he shouted to his reflection.

"Good-bye, my love!" Echo cried to Narcissus from her cave deep in the woods.

Then Narcissus took his last breath.

After he died, the water nymphs and wood nymphs searched for his body. But all they found was a magnificently beautiful flower beside the hidden pool where the youth had once yearned for his own reflection. The flower had white petals and a yellow center, and from that time on, it was called Narcissus.

And alas, poor Echo, desolate after Narcissus's death, did not eat or sleep. As she lay forlornly in her cave, all her beauty faded away, and she became very thin until her voice was all that was left. Thereafter, the lonely voice of Echo was heard in the mountains, repeating the last words anyone said.

THE KIDNAPPING

The Story of Ceres
and Proserpina

ONE day Proserpina, the young maiden of spring, was picking wildflowers with her mother, Ceres, the goddess of grain. Entering the cool moist woods, Proserpina filled her basket with lilies and violets. But when she spied the white petals of the narcissus flower, she strayed far from her mother.

Just as Proserpina picked a beautiful narcissus, the earth began to rumble. Suddenly the ground cracked open, splitting fern beds and ripping flowers and trees from their roots. Then out of the dark depths sprang Pluto, god of the underworld.

Standing up in his black chariot, Pluto ferociously drove his stallions toward Proserpina. The maiden screamed for her mother, but Ceres was far away and could not save her.

Pluto grabbed Proserpina and drove his chariot back into the earth. Then the ground closed up again, leaving not even a seam.

When the mountains echoed with Proserpina's screams, her mother rushed into the woods, but it was too late — her daughter had disappeared.

Beside herself with grief, Ceres began searching for her kidnapped daughter in every land. For nine days the goddess did not rest, but carried two torches through the cold nights, searching for Proserpina.

On the tenth day, Hecate, goddess of the dark of the moon, came to Ceres. Holding up a lantern, the shrouded goddess said, "I also heard your daughter's screams, but I didn't see her. Let us fly to Helios, the sun god, and ask him what happened."

Ceres and Hecate flew to Helios, the sun god; and weeping, Ceres asked Helios if he'd seen her daughter while he was shining down upon the woods.

"I pity you, Ceres," said Helios, "for I know what it is to lose a child. But I know the truth. Pluto wanted Proserpina for his wife, so he asked his brother, Jupiter, to give him permission to kidnap her. Jupiter gave his consent, and now your daughter reigns over the land of the dead with Pluto."

Ceres screamed in rage and thrust her fist toward Mount Olympus, cursing Jupiter for aiding in the kidnapping of his own daughter. Then she returned to earth, disguised as an old woman, and began wandering from town to town.

One day as she rested by a well, Ceres watched four princesses gathering water. Remembering her own daughter, she began to weep.

"Where are you from, old woman?" one princess asked.

"I was kidnapped by pirates, and I escaped," said Ceres. "Now I know not where I am."

Feeling pity for her, the princesses brought Ceres home to their palace. At the palace, their mother, the queen, took an immediate liking to Ceres when she noticied how good she was with her baby son the prince. When she asked Ceres if she would live with them and be his nurse, the goddess gladly consented.

Ceres grew deeply fond of the child. The thought that he would someday grow old and die was too much for her to bear. So she decided to change him from a mortal to a god. Every night, when everyone else was asleep, she poured a magic liquid on the body of the baby prince and held him in a fire. Soon the prince began to look like a god; everyone was amazed at his beauty and strength. The queen, disturbed by the changes in her child, hid in the nursery and watched Ceres and the boy. And when she saw Ceres place the child into the fire, she screamed for help.

"Stupid woman!" shouted Ceres, snatching the baby from the fire. "I was going to make your son a god! He would have lived forever! Now he'll be a mere mortal and die like the rest of you!"

The king and queen then realized that the boy's nurse was Ceres, the powerful goddess of grain, and they were terrified.

"I will only forgive you," said Ceres, "if you build a great temple in my honor. Then I will teach your people the secret rites to help the corn grow."

At dawn the king ordered a great temple be built for the goddess. But after the temple was completed, Ceres did not reveal the secret rites. Instead she sat by herself all day, grieving for her kidnapped daughter. She was in such deep mourning that everything on earth stopped growing. It was a terrible year — there was no food, and people and animals began to starve.

Jupiter grew worried — if Ceres caused the people on earth to die, there would be no more gifts and offerings for him. Finally he sent gods from Mount Olympus to speak with her.

The gods came to Ceres and offered her gifts and pleaded with her to make the earth fertile again.

"I never will," she said, "not unless my daughter is returned safely to me."

Jupiter had no choice but to bid his son, Mercury, the messenger god, to return Proserpina to her mother.

Wandering the underworld, Mercury passed through dark smoky

caverns filled with ghosts and phantoms, until he came to the misty throne room of Pluto and Proserpina. Though the maiden was still frightened, she had grown accustomed to her new home and had almost forgotten her life on earth.

"Your brother, Jupiter, has ordered you to return Proserpina to her mother," Mercury told Pluto. "Otherwise, Ceres will destroy the earth."

Pluto knew he could not disobey Jupiter, but he didn't want his wife to leave forever, so he said, "She can go. But first, we must be alone."

When Mercury left, Pluto spoke softly to Proserpina: "If you stay, you'll be queen of the underworld, and the dead will give you great honors."

As Proserpina stared into the eyes of the king of the dead, she dimly remembered the joy of her mother's love. She remembered wildflowers in the woods and open sunlit meadows. "I would rather return," she whispered.

Pluto sighed, then said, "All right, go. But before you leave, eat this small seed of the pomegranate fruit. It is the food of the underworld — it will bring you good luck."

Proserpina ate the tiny seed. Then Pluto's black chariot carried her and Mercury away. The two stallions burst through the dry ground of earth — then galloped over the barren countryside to the temple where Ceres mourned for her daughter.

When Ceres saw her daughter coming, she ran down the hillside, and Proserpina sprang from the chariot into her mother's arms. All day the two talked excitedly of what had happened during their separation, but when Proserpina told Ceres about eating the pomegranate seed, the goddess hid her face and moaned in anguish.

"What have I done?" cried Proserpina.

"You have eaten the sacred food of the underworld," said Ceres. "Now you must return for half of every year to live with Pluto, your husband."

And this is how the seasons began — for when fall and winter come, the earth grows cold and barren because Proserpina lives in the underworld with Pluto, and her mother mourns. But when her daughter comes back to her, Ceres, goddess of grain, turns the world to spring and summer: The corn grows, and everything flowers again.

THE GREAT BEAR

The Story of Callisto
and Arcus

 NE day Jupiter, god of the skies, fell in love with a lovely forest maiden named Callisto. Later, when Jupiter's jealous wife, Juno, heard that Callisto had given birth to Arcus, Jupiter's son, she flew into a terrible rage. The goddess quickly descended from Mount Olympus and searched the woods until she found Callisto playing under a tree with her small child.

When Callisto saw Juno, she cried out in fear, for all mortals knew about Juno's jealous rages.

"So, your beauty has captivated my husband!" Juno shouted. "Well, let's see how he likes you *this way*!"

As Callisto begged forgiveness, her skin became covered with coarse black hair. Her hands and feet turned to giant paws with sharp claws springing from them. Her mouth became filled with huge terrible teeth, and her voice turned into a deep growl — for Juno had changed the lovely maiden into a ferocious-looking bear.

Callisto still loved her small son, but as she lumbered toward him, he screamed in fear. Then the nymphs rushed from the woods and snatched the boy away from the giant bear.

Everyone was afraid of Callisto now that she was a huge black bear. No one knew that she was just as kind and loving as she'd always been. Hunted by men and dogs, she was forced to wander the woods and hide. She also fled from other wild animals — even bears like herself — for she didn't know how to fight, and she had no desire to learn.

At first Callisto tried to stay close to the hut where her son now lived with his new parents. Whenever Arcus took solitary walks, she lumbered close by, staying hidden among the trees. And at dawn, she crept to his window and watched him sleeping. Arcus often told his new parents that he was being watched by a giant black bear, but they told him he was only dreaming.

The great bear, pursued more and more by hunters and dogs, was finally forced to hide deep in the woods, far from her child.

But one winter night, many years later, the bear had a dream about Arcus, her son; and when she woke, she deeply yearned for him. As soon as spring came, she left her cave in the forest and journeyed back to the land where she had once lived.

One twilight, as the bear wandered the familiar woods, remembering her past, she came upon a young hunter aiming his arrow at a distant bird. She froze — for she instantly knew that this was Arcus, her son by Jupiter. Overcome with love for the boy, the bear watched him pull back his bowstring and shoot the arrow at the bird.

When the arrow missed, the bear was glad. Since she was a wild animal herself, she wanted all creatures to escape from hunters. But then Arcus turned and saw the bear watching him, and his muscles became taut with fear. Slowly he raised his bow and aimed his arrow directly at the bear. Unable to move, the bear only stared at her son with mute grief.

But just at that moment, Jupiter happened to look down upon the earth from Mount Olympus, and he saw what was about to happen. He moved quickly to save the bear, for he had once loved her very much when she'd been a young maiden. As fast as a lightning bolt, he swept down from his mountain, snatched Callisto, and hurled her into the night sky. Then Jupiter grabbed Arcus and hurled him also into the heavens where he became a small bear beside his mother.

Then *both* bears turned into stars. And thereafter, they lived together in the sky and were known as the Great Bear and the Little Bear constellations. When jealous Juno discovered them, however, she commanded Neptune, god of the sea, to forbid the two bears to descend into the ocean like the other stars. For this reason, the Great Bear and Little Bear are the only two constellations that never set below the horizon.

JOURNEY
TO THE UNDERWORLD

The Story of Orpheus and Eurydice

"SHHH — " whispered the wind. The autumn trees were still; the birds held their song — for Orpheus, the greatest mortal musician, was singing his wedding vows to the beautiful maiden, Eurydice.

After the ceremony, all of nature watched the couple wander through a great open field. But suddenly Eurydice cried out — then fell to the ground as a poisonous snake slithered away through the grass. Orpheus screamed his wife's name and tried to embrace her, but it was too late. The snake's poison had filled her veins, and her gentle spirit had descended into the underworld.

After Eurydice died, Orpheus was beside himself with grief. Even the trees and wild animals mourned with him as he sang about his loss. When he could bear his pain no longer, he decided to journey to the underworld to look for Eurydice.

A ferryman carried Orpheus across the murky swamp of the river Styx, the dark river that bordered the land of the living and the dead. Then Orpheus held a torch as he entered a pitch-black region where horrible sounds echoed through a cavernous landscape, and buried ghosts and phantom dwellers floated by.

Groping his way down a dark, sloping passage, Orpheus passed the Furies, with their ravaged faces and great bodies. Then he passed Cerberus, the three-headed watchdog who guarded the palace of Pluto and Proserpina, rulers of the dead.

When Orpheus stood before the king and queen in their misty throne room, he fell to his knees.

"Welcome, Orpheus," Pluto said. "Rise and sing to us about why you have come."

Orpheus began playing his lyre, and in a beautiful voice he sang a song about his lost love:

> *Allow her to return with me.*
> *She'll come to you eventually.*
> *Do not give her —*
> *but lend her to me, please.*

As Orpheus sang, his beautiful voice caused iron tears to stream down Pluto's cheeks. The pale ghosts and phantom dwellers began to weep — tears fell from the dark holes of their eyes. And tears fell from the eyes of the Furies who hung their tortured heads and cried for the first time in their lives. Even the three-headed dog wept, and the ferryman of the river Styx wept. Everyone stopped whatever they were doing in the dark passages below the earth and wept for Orpheus and Eurydice.

After Pluto and Proserpina wiped their tears, they called for Orpheus's bride. But they wept again when Eurydice stepped into the throne room, limping from her fatal wound and cried out, "Orpheus, you have come for me!"

Orpheus held his wife closely; and as he buried his face against her, he could smell the sweet flowers still woven through her hair.

"Eurydice may return with you," said Pluto, "but only on one condition: that you *not* look back at her on your way out of the underworld. You must trust her to follow you. Until you are both on earth, you must not look back — or your journey will have been in vain."

Orpheus gladly consented to Pluto's condition, for it seemed a simple one. Then he thanked the rulers of the dead and began his trek up the steep, dark path back to earth, with Eurydice following him.

Determined not to look back, Orpheus led his bride past the three-headed watchdog and the snake-haired Furies, then through the dismal, damp passages, passing ghosts and phantoms. As the smoke rose from his torch into the pitch-black air, and the cavern filled with horrible cries, he longed to look back and make certain Eurydice was all right; but he remembered Pluto's warning and resisted the temptation.

Finally, after the ferryman had carried him across the murky river Styx, Orpheus saw light streaming into the entrance of the underworld. He waited till he had leapt out of the dark cavern of death — then he turned and looked back at Eurydice.

But Orpheus had forgotten that Pluto had said they must *both* be out of the underworld before he could look at her again, so just as his eyes fastened on Eurydice's gentle, loving face, she uttered, "Farewell," — then vanished back into the dark depths.

Orpheus rushed after Eurydice, but ghostly phantoms barred his way. He begged the ferryman to take him back to the land of the dead, but the ferryman thrust him aside. It was no use, he could not return, and Eurydice could not join him. She had disappeared into the underworld for the second time — and this time, forever.

Orpheus left the bank of the river Styx and dragged himself to the top of a green, windswept hill where he wept and moaned.

But his moaning soon turned into lovely, mournful singing; and as he sang, the trees began moving toward him. An oak with sturdy branches bowed with acorns, a willow that grew by the river, a shining silver fir, a green boxwood, a red maple, a lime, a laurel, a linden — all these trees protected Orpheus from the harsh winds and burning sunlight as they listened mutely to his sad and beautiful song.

THE GOLDEN APPLES

The Story of Atalanta
and Hippomenes

ONG ago a baby girl named Atalanta was left on a wild mountainside because her father had wanted a boy instead of a girl. A kind bear discovered the tiny girl and nursed her and cared for her. And as Atalanta grew up, she lived as the bears lived: eating wild honey and berries and hunting in the woods. Finally as a young woman on her own, she became a follower of Diana, the goddess of wild things. Preferring to live on her own, Atalanta blissfully roamed the shadowy woods and sunlit fields.

The god Apollo agreed with Atalanta's choice to be alone. "You must never marry," he told her one day. "If you do, you will surely lose your own identity."

In spite of her decision never to marry, Atalanta was pursued by many suitors. As men watched her run through the fields and forest, they were struck by her beauty and grace.

Angry at the men for bothering her, Atalanta figured out how to keep them away. "I'll race anyone who wants to marry me!" she announced to the daily throng that pursued her. "Whoever is so swift that he can outrun me will receive the prize of my hand in marriage! But whomever I beat — will die."

Atalanta was certain these harsh conditions would discourage everyone from wanting to marry her. But she was wrong. Her strength and grace were so compelling that many men volunteered to race against her — and all of them lost their lives.

One day, a young stranger, wandering through the countryside, stopped to join a crowd that was watching a race between Atalanta and one of her suitors. When Hippomenes realized the terms of the contest, he was appalled. "No person could be worth such a risk!" he exclaimed. "Only an idiot would try to win her for his wife!"

But when Atalanta sped by, and Hippomenes saw her wild hair flying back from her ivory shoulders and her strong body moving as gracefully as a gazelle, even he was overwhelmed with the desire to be her husband.

"Forgive me," he said to the panting loser being taken away to his death. "I did not know what a prize she was."

When Atalanta was crowned with the wreath of victory, Hippomenes stepped forward boldly and spoke to her before the crowd. "Why do you race against men so slow?" he asked. "Why not race against me? If I defeat you, you will not be disgraced, for I am the great-grandson of Neptune, god of the seas!"

"And if I beat you?" Atalanta asked.

"If you beat me . . . you will certainly have something to boast about!"

As Atalanta stared at the proud young man, she wondered why the gods would wish one as young and bold as Hippomenes to die. And for the first time, she felt she might rather lose than win. Inexperienced in matters of the heart, she did not realize she was falling in love. "Go, stranger," she said softly. "I'm not worth the loss of your life."

But the crowd, sensing a tremendous race might be about to

take place, cheered wildly, urging the two to compete. And since Hippomenes eagerly sought the same, Atalanta was forced to give in. With a heavy heart, she consented to race the young man the next day.

In the pink twilight, alone in the hills, Hippomenes prayed to Venus, the goddess of love and beauty. He asked for help in his race against Atalanta. When Venus heard Hippomenes's prayer, she was only too glad to help him, for she wished to punish the young huntress for despising love.

As if in a dream, Venus led Hippomenes to a mighty tree in the middle of an open field. The tree shimmered with golden leaves and golden apples. Venus told Hippomenes to pluck three of the apples from the tree, and then she told him how to use the apples in his race against Atalanta.

The crowd roared as Atalanta and Hippomenes crouched at the starting line. Under his tunic, Hippomenes hid his three golden apples. When the trumpets sounded, the two shot forward and ran so fast that their bare feet barely touched the sand. They looked as if they could run over the surface of the sea without getting their feet wet — or skim over fields of corn without even bending the stalks.

The crowd cheered for Hippomenes, but Atalanta rushed ahead of him and stayed in the lead. When Hippomenes began to pant, and his chest felt as if it might burst open, he pulled one of the golden apples out from under his tunic and tossed it toward Atalanta.

The gleaming apple hit the sand and rolled across Atalanta's path. She left her course and chased after the glittering ball, and Hippomenes gained the lead. The crowd screamed with joy; but after Atalanta picked up the golden apple, she quickly made up for her delay and scooted ahead of Hippomenes.

Hippomenes tossed another golden apple. Again, Atalanta left her course, picked up the apple, then overtook Hippomenes.

As Hippomenes pulled out his third golden apple, he realized this was his last chance. He reared back his arm and hurled the apple as far as he could into a field.

Atalanta watched the golden ball fly through the air; and she hesitated, wondering whether or not she should run after it. Just as she decided not to, Venus touched her heart, prompting her to abandon her course and rush after the glittering apple.

Atalanta took off into the field after the golden apple — and Hippomenes sped toward the finish line.

Hippomenes won Atalanta for his bride, but then he made a terrible mistake: He neglected to offer gifts to Venus to thank her for helping him.

Enraged by his ingratitude, the goddess of love and beauty called upon the moon goddess, Diana, and told her to punish Hippomenes and Atalanta.

As the moon goddess studied the two proud lovers hunting in the woods and fields, she admired their strength and valor, and she decided to turn them into the animals they most resembled.

One night as Atalanta and Hippomenes lay side by side under the moonlight, changes began to happen to their bodies. They grew rough amber coats, and stiff, long claws. And when dawn came, they woke and growled at the early light. Then the thick tails of the two mighty lions swept the ground as they began hunting for their breakfast.

From then on, Atalanta and Hippomenes lived together as lions deep in the woods, and only the moon goddess could tame them.

THE FOUR TASKS

The Story of Cupid
and Psyche

LONG ago a king and queen had three lovely daughters. The two older ones were just a bit above ordinary. But the youngest, named Psyche, was the fairest and brightest girl in the kingdom. People began to desert the altars of Venus, the goddess of love and beauty, and worship Psyche instead. In fact, some were even beginning to call Psyche the second Venus.

Venus, furious about Psyche's fame, ordered her son Cupid to wound the princess with one of his arrows. "Avenge your mother!" she cried. "Make Psyche fall in love with the vilest of men — the most miserable and meanest beast you can find!"

Cupid set out at once to do his mother's bidding. But when the god of love laid eyes on the fair maiden, he accidently pricked his own finger with one of his arrows — and he himself fell in love with Psyche.

Tormented by his sudden passion, Cupid immediately flew to Apollo, the god of light and truth, and asked for his help.

Soon afterwards all of Psyche's admirers mysteriously vanished. Her father couldn't understand why his daughter's suitors had stopped calling. Fearing the gods might be angry with him, he asked Apollo for advice.

"Perhaps it has been decreed your daughter is to marry a god," Apollo said. "Leave her alone on top of a mountain, and soon you will find out if a god wants her for his wife."

When Psyche's father returned home and reported what Apollo had said, a cry of grief went up from the household, for they all knew they would soon lose their beautiful Psyche. But since the commands of the gods must always be obeyed, the king and queen prepared their daughter for her lonely exile.

The whole city lit torches. And to the sound of a lonely flute, people chanted a funeral hymn as they escorted the beautiful princess up a steep mountain. When they reached the topmost peak, Psyche spoke to her family and friends: "Fear not. Do not torment yourself with grief, but leave me now to meet my fate."

After her brave words, everyone bid her good-bye; and as they filed down the mountainside, their torches were nearly extinguished by their tears.

Psyche also cried until she finally fell asleep on the deserted mountaintop. But while she slept, the gentle West Wind lifted her up and bore her down to a flowery plateau. And in the morning, when she woke, she found herself lying in a bed of grass before a great palace that had a roof of ivory and columns of gold. A chorus of sweet music filled the air, and the soft voices of invisible beings whispered in her ear, "All of this is yours now."

Psyche wandered about the golden, gleaming palace. She bathed herself in refreshing spring waters and ate a wonderful dinner, which invisible hands placed before her.

During the night, Cupid came to her. "You are my wife," he said in the dark. "I love you more than anything. But I must ask that you never try to look upon my face. I will only visit you in the night; but our nights will be glorious and filled with joy."

When Psyche asked why she could not look at him, Cupid only said, "Honor my request, for if you look upon me, we will be separated forever." Actually Cupid was afraid that if Psyche discovered he was the son of Venus, she would adore him as a god, rather than love him as an equal.

Psyche loved her nightly visits with Cupid, though during the day she was sad and lonely. One night, she asked her husband to allow her to send for her two older sisters.

"If they come here, it will be the beginning of our doom," Cupid said.

"Oh, no! Please, let them come!" Psyche begged. "If you won't allow me to see you, at least allow me to see my sisters!"

It saddened Cupid to hear these words, so he ordered the West Wind to bring Psyche's older sisters to her.

When the sisters arrived at the palace, they were overjoyed to find Psyche alive and well. But as soon as they began to look about and note the splendor in which she lived, they grew envious. By the time they returned home, they were in a jealous rage because their own husbands were not as wealthy as Psyche's.

On their second visit to the palace, the sisters demanded to meet Psyche's husband.

"I'm afraid I cannot let you see him," she said.

"Why? Is he so ugly that you are ashamed?"

"No, he can't allow himself to be seen. Even I have not seen him in the daylight."

"What?" her sisters screamed.

"I try not to mind," said Psyche. "He's very gentle and kind, and he seems to love me more than life itself."

The two sisters grew more envious than ever when they heard

how much Psyche's husband loved her. When they returned home, they tore their hair and wailed with sorrow because their own husbands were cold and unkind.

The sisters grew so jealous of Psyche, they decided to spoil her happiness. The next time they came to the palace, one said, "We don't believe your husband is so wonderful after all."

"Oh, but he is," said Psyche.

"Oh, but he is not!" said the other sister. "We've been to an oracle, and she said your husband is a loathsome, horrible monster! And that's why he won't let you look upon him!"

"No! That's not true!" cried Psyche.

"It is! And what's more — she said he's just waiting for you to have his child, and then he plans to kill you!"

"No! No!" Psyche wept.

But finally her sisters persuaded her that her husband was indeed a horrible monster; and they convinced her that in the night, she must hold a lantern above him — and then cut off his head.

In the dark, all was quiet, except for the sound of Cupid's soft breathing as he slept. Psyche trembled as she slipped from their bed and fetched the oil lamp and knife she'd hidden earlier.

When she returned to bed, Psyche lit her lamp, then slowly lifted it above Cupid's head. She was stunned to see the flushed, shining face of Venus's son. Even her lamplight burned brighter with joy as it beheld the beautiful god.

In a daze, Psyche gently touched Cupid's golden curls and his white, shining wings and his quiver of arrows. When she touched one of his arrows, she pricked herself — and fell deeply in love with the god of love. Psyche felt such rapture she nearly swooned to the floor. As she caught herself, a drop of oil fell from her lamp onto Cupid's shoulder.

Cupid woke up. When he saw Psyche staring wide-eyed at him, holding a knife in her hand, a look of sadness crossed his face. "My love, were you afraid that I was a hideous monster?"

Before Psyche could answer, he said, "There can be no love if there is not trust. I will never come to you again." And with those sad words, he started to fly away.

Crying out in grief, Psyche grabbed onto Cupid and clung to him as he soared high into the sky. But soon, overcome with weariness, she fell to the ground. Then she lay alone in the cold dark night, wishing she could die.

Thereafter, Psyche wandered the earth, searching for her lost husband. She didn't know that Cupid was as sad as she; and that he lay in bed at his mother's palace, wounded by his love for her.

Psyche desperately sought help from all the gods and goddesses, but none wished to incur the wrath of Venus. Only Ceres, the goddess of grain would give her counsel.

"Seek Venus and beg her forgiveness," Ceres advised, "for her son now lies in her palace, mourning for you. And Venus tires of caring for him. Beg her to unite the two of you again."

But Venus let out a wild shriek when she saw Psyche humbly standing on her doorstep. The great goddess ordered her handmaidens Trouble and Sorrow to fall upon the girl and tear her clothes and pull her hair.

When the dreadful attack was over, Venus smiled at Psyche who lay trembling on the ground. "Now, you want to see my son? Don't you know he loathes you and wishes to never lay eyes upon you again? Really, you are such a plain and unfortunate creature, I almost take pity on you. Perhaps I should train you to be more fitting for a god."

Venus then gave Psyche a task to perform. She led the girl to

61

a storehouse filled with grains of many kinds. "Sort all these by evening," she said. And with that, she disappeared.

As Psyche stared hopelessly at the piles of barley, lentils, and poppy seeds, an amazing thing began to happen. An army of ants assembled; and within minutes, waves of ants crawled up the piles of grain. Each ant carried one tiny seed at a time — until all the seeds were sorted into three different piles.

When Venus returned at nightfall, she flew into a rage. "Some one has helped you!" she shrieked. "In the morning I demand you complete another task!" Then Venus threw Psyche a piece of hard black bread and left her to sleep on the cold threshing floor.

The next morning, Venus pushed Psyche out into the rosy dawn. "Go to the pasture beside the flowing stream!" the goddess said. "There live the fierce rams with golden wool! Gather some of their fleece — and then you might be a person worthy of my son's love!"

Psyche stood by the flowing stream that bordered the pasture where the wild rams grazed. As she watched the beasts fight with one another, she knew she could never get near their wool without being killed. She felt such despair she wanted to drown herself in the stream.

But then a green swaying reed began to whisper melodically, "Do not slay yourself, Psyche. Nor approach those terrible sheep. In the noonday heat, when the sheep are napping, slip into the pasture and pick the golden wool that clings to the sharp briars and thorny bushes."

At noontime when the drowsy rams lay down for a nap, Psyche crossed the stream and crept into the pasture. And within a short time, she had gathered all the golden wool that clung to the twigs and briars.

When Venus saw Psyche's wool, she smiled bitterly. "Someone

must be helping you," she said, and she gave her yet another task. This time she wanted Psyche to fill a crystal goblet with icy mountain water from the mouth of the Stygian river.

Psyche took the goblet from Venus and began climbing the craggy rocks of the mountain. But when she got near the top, she realized this was the worst task yet, for the rocks near the mouth of the river were hopelessly steep and slippery. Just as she decided to fling herself off the mountain, an eagle flew over.

"Wait!" the eagle cried. "Give me the crystal goblet, and I will fly to the mouth of the black river and get water for you!"

Psyche gave her goblet to the eagle, and he held the vessel tightly with his fierce jaws as he flew to the mountain peak. After he'd filled the vessel and returned it to Psyche, she carried the dark water back to Venus.

When Psyche handed the goblet to Venus, the goddess accused her of being a sorceress. Then she gave Psyche the cruelest task of all: She ordered her to carry a box to the underworld and ask Queen Proserpina for a small portion of her beauty.

Psyche knew this was the end, for never would she gain the courage to descend to the underworld, the terrifying land of the dead. With great despair, she climbed to the top of a high tower and prepared to hurl herself to her death.

But just as she was about to jump, the tower spoke: "What cowardice makes you give up now, Psyche? Be kind to yourself, and I will tell you how to reach the underworld and how to succeed in your quest."

After she promised not to kill herself, the tower told Psyche how to travel to the land of the dead. "Take two coins and two pieces of barley cake," the tower said. "A lame donkey driver will ask you for help, but you must refuse him.

"Then give one coin to Charon, the ferryman, and he will take you across the river Styx to the underworld. As you cross the water, the groping hand of a dying man will reach out to you, but you must turn away. You must also refuse to help three women weaving the threads of fate.

"When you come to Cerberus, the three-headed watchdog that guards the palace doors, give him a barley cake, and he will be friendly to you. Do all of this again on your way out. But most importantly, when you carry the box of beauty from Proserpina back to Venus, *do not open it* — whatever you do, *do not open the beauty box!*"

Psyche did as the tower told her, until finally she had secured the box of beauty from Proserpina, queen of the dead. Then she repeated her actions as she left the underworld: She gave Cerberus a cake on her way out of the palace; she gave Charon a coin to take her across the river Styx; and she refused to stop for any who tried to ensnare her with cries for help.

But when Psyche was close to Venus's palace, a burning curiosity overtook her. She was dying to open the box and use a small portion of Proserpina's beauty.

Psyche gingerly lifted the lid of the box. But she did not find beauty inside — instead, she found a deadly sleep; and as the sleep overtook her, she crumpled to the road.

Meanwhile Cupid had escaped out the window of his palace room; and as he was flying over the earth, searching for Psyche, he saw her lying unconscious beside the road.

Cupid hastened down to her and quickly gathered the sleep from her body and closed it back inside the box. Then he woke Psyche with a kiss.

Before Venus could catch them, Cupid lifted Psyche from the ground and carried her high into the heavens to Mount Olympus to the home of Jupiter, god of the skies; and he bid Jupiter to officially marry them.

After Jupiter married Cupid and Psyche, all of Mount Olympus celebrated the couple — except for Venus, of course. She raged about for weeks. But within the year, the aging goddess became the grandmother of a beautiful baby girl named Bliss.

THE MYSTERIOUS
VISITORS

The Story of Baucis and Philemon

LONG ago, two old mortals named Baucis and Philemon had just finished their midday meal when they heard someone knocking on the door. They happily rushed to the front of their tiny thatched cottage, for as much as they loved each other, they loved having visitors. When they threw open the door, there, standing before them, were two tall strangers. One was a very strong-looking bearded man, the other was an impish-looking young man.

"We've traveled from far away," said the bearded man in a beautiful deep voice. "Is it possible we might rest a while in your home?"

"Come in, come in!" said Baucis, and she held the door as the two visitors ducked their heads and entered the tiny cottage.

Philemon rushed to the fire and raked the coals. He added leaves and bark and blew hard to make a cheerful blaze. Baucis put a copper kettle over the flames, then scurried around the kitchen to make some soup.

While they worked, the old couple chatted happily with their visitors, for they wanted them to feel at home.

As Baucis prepared the table, Philemon bathed the feet of the visitors and dried them with towels. Then Baucis served many earthenware dishes filled with cabbage and bacon, black olives, cherries soaked in wine, garden salad with endive and radishes, milk-white honeycomb, nuts, figs, dates, plums, grapes fresh from the vine, and delicious red apples.

After Philemon poured wine into beech goblets, he stood by the table and wrung his old gnarled hands. "Please forgive us, gentlemen," he said, "for giving you so little." Then before the visitors could protest, Baucis told Philemon to offer their visitors their only goose!

Tears filled Philemon's eyes, for he and Baucis had a strong affection for their old goose. They thought of the goose as being somewhat the guardian of their estate. But the old man nodded and agreed good-naturedly. Then he hurried outside to catch the old gander.

The two visitors stood at the cottage door and watched the old couple exhaust themselves as they dashed about their dirt yard, trying to catch the skinny goose.

Just as the goose sought refuge behind the visitors, the bearded man held up his hand and said, "Stop! Don't kill your only goose!"

When Baucis and Philemon returned to the cottage, the younger stranger said, "We are not mortals. We are gods come down from Mount Olympus. I am Mercury, and this is my father, Jupiter."

Baucis and Philemon let out cries of disbelief. They were astounded that Jupiter, greatest of all the gods on Mount Olympus, was in their cottage! And Mercury, his son, the messenger god who could fly through the air! Suddenly the mysterious visitors were bathed in a shimmering light, and they seemed to grow larger than life. Awestruck and frightened, Baucis and Philemon backed against their wall.

Jupiter urged them not to be afraid, but to leave their house immediately and come with him and Mercury to Mount Olympus.

"But why?" stammered Philemon.

"Your wicked countrymen will soon be destroyed. Mercury and I came to earth to test the warmth and hospitality of mortals. We visited hundreds of homes, but no one was friendly to us — except the two of you."

Baucis and Philemon quickly gathered a small bundle of their things. Then they leaned on their walking sticks as they followed Jupiter and Mercury up a steep hill.

When the four reached the top of the hill, they looked down and saw water covering the land below. Baucis and Philemon wept for their neighbors. But suddenly they gasped when they saw their cottage floating on top of the water. Before everyone's eyes, the cottage changed into a gleaming temple: Its wooden pillars became shining marble columns. The straw thatch became gold; the doors, wondrously carved gates; and the rough wooden floors, white marble.

Then Jupiter told Baucis and Philemon to make a wish, for he wanted to repay them for their kindness and generosity.

They thought for a while, then said, "We would like to be keepers of your temple that was once our cottage. And we would like to die together someday, so that one of us is not left behind without the other."

"Your wish shall be granted," said Jupiter.

So Baucis and Philemon became the keepers of Jupiter's temple, and they lived many more happy years together. Then one day, each began to see changes in the other: Tree bark began growing on their shoulders; their arms began sprouting forth bright green leaves; their feet changed into new roots. Baucis was slowly turning into a linden tree, and Philemon, to an oak.

Their foliage spread daily until finally one evening, they

whispered to one another, "Farewell, my dear!" "Farewell!" And then the bark closed over their mouths.

After Baucis and Philemon turned into trees, their countrymen on earth often showed strangers the great oak and linden that grew from only one trunk; and they always recited a line when they hung wreaths on the two trees:

Those who care for the gods
someday become gods
themselves.

GODS, GODDESSES
AND MORTALS

THE Titans were the first gods of the universe. Saturn, ruler of the Titans, was the father of Jupiter, Neptune, Pluto, Juno, Ceres, and Vesta. When Saturn's children joined forces against him, he was compelled to yield his throne to his son, Jupiter. Thereafter, Jupiter was ruler of all the gods; and since he lived on top of a mountain called Mount Olympus, he and his family were called the Olympians.

The major Greek gods and goddesses of Mount Olympus were later adopted by the Romans. The myths in this collection use their Roman names; their Greek names are in parenthesis.

The Olympians, Major Gods and Goddesses

Jupiter (Zeus) — son of Saturn, ruler of the Olympian gods, god of the skies

Neptune (Poseidon) — Jupiter's brother, god of the sea

Pluto (Hades) — Jupiter's brother, god of the underworld

Juno (Hera) — Jupiter's sister and wife, goddess of marriage

Ceres (Demeter) — Jupiter's sister, mother of Proserpina, goddess of grain

Vesta (Hestia) — Jupiter's sister, goddess of the hearth

Minerva (Athena) — Jupiter's daughter, goddess of handicrafts, goddess of the city, protector of civilized life, goddess of wisdom, goddess of battle

Apollo (Apollo) — Jupiter's son, god of light and truth

Diana (Artemis) — Jupiter's daughter, Apollo's twin sister, goddess of wild things, the huntress goddess, the moon goddess

Mercury (Hermes) — Jupiter's son, messenger god, trickster god

Mars (Ares) — Jupiter and Hera's son, god of war

Vulcan (Hephaestus) — Hera's son, Venus's husband, god of fire

Bacchus (Dionysus) — Jupiter's son, god of wine

Proserpina (Persephone) — Jupiter's niece, daughter of Ceres, Pluto's wife, maiden of spring, queen of the underworld

Venus (Aphrodite) — goddess of love and beauty, sprung from the foam of the sea

Cupid (Eros) — Venus's son, god of love

Other Gods and Goddesses

Besides the major gods and goddesses of Mount Olympus, there were many other minor Greek gods and goddesses. Some who appear in this collection are:

Helios — a Titan, the sun god

Iris — Juno's messenger, goddess of the rainbow

Sleep — god of slumber

Morpheus — one of Sleep's thousand sons; god of dreams

Peneas — river god, father of the nymph Daphne

Hecate — goddess of the dark of the moon

Pan — Mercury's son, the shepherds' god, a goat-man

Nymphs — companions of Pan, lovely maiden goddesses of the woods, seas, and mountains; Daphne and Echo are nymphs.

Mortals

Mortals were ordinary people who did not live forever. Though one of their parents might have been a god or goddess, that did not guarantee they would be one. The mortals in this collection of myths are:

Phaeton	Narcissus	Atalanta
King Midas	Callisto	Hippomenes
Ceyx	Arcus	Psyche
Alcyone	Orpheus	Baucis
Arachne	Eurydice	Philemon

Other Names to Know

Aeolus — king of the winds, viceroy of the gods

Cerberus — three-headed watchdog of the underworld; permits spirits to enter, but not to leave

Charon — aged boatman who ferries souls of the dead to the underworld

Furies — live in underworld, punish evildoers

Mount Olympus — mythical heavenly mountaintop above the earth, home of Jupiter and his family

Oracle — A person who possesses great knowledge and can look into the future; King Ceyx was on his way to consult an oracle about his country's problem

Pactolus River — river whose sands were turned to gold by King Midas

River Styx — river of the underworld; river of oaths by which gods swear

Underworld — the land of the dead ruled by Pluto and Proserpina

MODERN WORDS
WITH GREEK ORIGINS

MANY words we use today have their origins in the Greek myths. The following list shows examples:

arachnid — is the term that scientists use to describe the spider family; originates from Arachne, the girl whom Minerva turned into a spider

aeolian harp — is a harp sounded by the wind; name derived from Aeolus, king of the winds

cereal — breakfast food of grains; derived from Ceres, goddess of grain

cupidity — means strong desire; derived from Cupid, the god of love

halcyon — means peaceful and calm; derived from *Alcyone*, daughter of the wind king, who turned into a seagull

helium — is an inert, light gas derived from Helios, god of the sun

iridescent — means a rainbowlike display of colors; the word is derived from Iris, the goddess of the rainbow.

mercury — silver-white metallic element, also called quicksilver; planet nearest the sun; derived from Mercury, Jupiter's son

morphine — medicine used to relieve pain and induce sleep; derived from Morpheus, god of dreams

narcissus — the name of a family of flowers which includes jonquils and daffodils

narcissist — a person who is inordinately absorbed in himself; both derived from Narcissus, the youth who fell in love with his own reflection

Olympics — the name of the world-famous athletic games comes from Mount Olympus, home of the major Greek gods and goddesses

phaeton — an open four-wheeled carriage used in the 19th century; derived from Phaeton, who drove his father's sun chariot

pluton — is rock formed far below the earth's surface; derived from Pluto, the god of the underworld

Stygian — derived from the river Styx, is used to describe anything from the underworld; dark and gloomy

WHO WROTE
THE GREEK MYTHS?

ANY great Greek and Latin poets created the myths, starting with the Greek poet Homer, who lived 3,000 years ago. All the myths in this collection were retold or invented by the Latin poet Ovid — with the exception of the story of Cupid and Psyche, which was first told in the second century by the Latin writer Apuleius.

Ovid lived in early Rome from 43 B.C. to 18 A.D. Drawing mostly from Homer and the Greek playwrights, he gathered 250 myths together in a collection called *Metamorphoses*, or *The Stories of Changing Forms*. Most of the stories involve transformation — or gods, goddesses, and mortals changing their shapes to become different things. It has been said that Ovid probably influenced Western literature more than any other ancient writer. Dante, Chaucer, Milton, Shakespeare, and many other great writers show traces of Ovid in their work.

BIBLIOGRAPHY

Bulfinch, Thomas, *Bulfinch's Mythology*, Doubleday & Company, Inc., 1968.

d'Aulaire, Ingri and Edgar Parin, *d'Aulaire's Book of Greek Myths*, Doubleday & Company, Inc., 1962.

Grant, Michael, *Myths of the Greeks and Romans*, New American Library, 1962.

Graves, Robert, *The Greek Myths*, Penguin Books, 1955.

Hamilton, Edith, *Mythology*, Little, Brown, & Company, 1940.

Humphries, Rolfe, translation of Ovid's *Metamorphoses*, Indiana University Press, 1955.

Innes, Mary M., translation of Ovid's *Metamorphoses*, Penguin Books, 1955.

INDEX

F

Furies (pursue and punish evildoers),
46, 47, 74

G

Great Bear (a constellation), 3, 4, 43
Greece, x
Greeks, ix-x

H

Halcyon days, 16, 75
Hecate (goddess of dark of the moon), 36
Helios (sun god), 1, 2, 3, 5, 6, 36, 73, 75
Hippomenes (a mortal; great-grandson of
Neptune), 52–54, 73
Homer (Greek poet), 77
Hours (two goddesses), 3, 6

I

Iris (goddess of the rainbow), 14–15,
73, 75

J

Juno (Jupiter's wife; goddess of marriage),
14, 29, 41, 43, 71

Jupiter (king of the gods; god of the skies),
2, 4, 5, 25, 29, 36, 37, 38, 41,
42–43, 65, 68–69, 71

L

Lethe (a river), 14
Little Bear (a constellation), 43

M

Mercury (messenger god), 37–38, 68, 69,
72, 76
Metamorphoses (book by Ovid), x, 77
Midas, King, 9–11, 73, 74
Minerva (goddess of weaving and
handicrafts), 19–21, 72
Morpheus (son of Sleep; god of dreams),
15, 73, 76
Mortals, 73
Mother Earth, 4, 5
Mount Olympus, x, 4, 15, 19, 20, 36, 37,
41, 42, 64–65, 68, 71, 74, 76
Myths, ix-x, 77

N

Narcissus (a beautiful youth), 29–32,
73, 76
Neptune (god of the seas), 43, 52, 71